Newport Public Library
This discarded book needs
a new home.
We hope you enjoy it.

For Marie
G.M.

Manufactured in Hong Kong in June 2017 by Paramount Printing

First Edition
21 20 19 18 17   5 4 3 2 1

Text © 2017 Thierry Robberecht
Illustrations © 2017 Grégoire Mabire
All rights reserved. No part of this book
may be reproduced by any means
whatsoever without written permission
from the publisher, except brief
portions quoted for purpose of
review.

Published by
Gibbs Smith
P.O. Box 667
Layton, Utah 84041

1.800.835.4993 orders
www.gibbs-smith.com

Gibbs Smith books are printed on paper
produced from sustainable PEFC-certified forest/
controlled wood source. Learn more at www.pefc.org.

Library of Congress Control Number: 2017932757
ISBN: 978-1-4236-4797-3

NEWPORT PUBLIC LIBRARY
NEWPORT, OREGON 97365

Thierry Robberecht

The Wolf
Who Fell Out
of a Book

Grégoire Mabire

GIBBS SMITH
TO ENRICH AND INSPIRE HUMANKIND

Zoe's library shelves were stuffed so full of books
that one day, a book fell to the ground,
and a wolf tumbled out of the story.

Inside the book, the wolf was scary,
with pitch-black fur and pointy teeth.
But in Zoe's room, a place he'd never been,
the wolf was all alone . . . and very afraid.

First he tried to find shelter
under his own book,
which had fallen from the shelf
into the shape of a tent.
The problem was a cat
who slept in Zoe's room . . .
a large cat who was
already licking his lips.

"Don't touch me,"
the wolf told him.
"In my book,
I am a scary wolf
and everyone
is afraid of me!"

"Perhaps," said the cat,
"but here, you're not in your book.
You're in Zoe's room, and this is my territory."

The wolf was so afraid that he tried to go back inside his book . . .

but a sheep kicked him out
because he arrived too early in the story.
"What are you already doing here?
You're much too early.
There's no wolf in this story yet.
Couldn't you just leave us alone to graze in peace?"

So he tried to enter the book through another page,
but there, other wolves scolded him, "Smart move, wise guy.
Now you arrive? When the story is finished?"

The cat was moving closer and closer to the wolf.
He would have to run away quickly!

So the wolf climbed up the shelves looking for a book
where he could hide. The shelves were tall, straight,
and steep like a cliff. The wolf nearly fell ten times.

Finally the wolf managed to reach the top shelf,
where he tried to get into the first book he saw.

It was a book about princesses,
and at the page where the wolf arrived,
the king was giving a grand ball at court.
"So sorry, Mister Wolf," the butler told him.
"For you to remain in this story, you must change.
Put on a tuxedo or a ball gown."
"A ball gown!" answered the wolf.
"And what if other wolves saw me?"

And so it was that the wolf
was kicked out of the book.
Outside, the cat was still waiting,
so the wolf jumped into another book.

In this book, the world was unlike anything he knew.
Suddenly he felt a presence behind him.
"My boy," said a dinosaur,
"you won't be able to stay in this book.
You've chosen the wrong time period.
Besides, it's dangerous for you here."

The animals in this story were enormous and scary.

Worried and a bit worse for wear,
the wolf quickly escaped from the book.

"Close that book tightly,"
the cat told him.
"I don't want any dinosaurs
in Zoe's room."

The wolf chose another book at random
and scrambled inside.

NEWPORT PUBLIC LIBRARY
NEWPORT, OREGON 97365

He found himself in a large forest.

"A forest. I like it," he said to himself.
He walked for a long time.

He saw a little girl dressed in red,
seated on a tree trunk, crying.

"What's the matter?" the wolf asked her.
"Why are you crying?"

"I'm on my way to bring some pancakes
and a bit of butter to my grandmother.
I was supposed to meet a wolf here,
but he hasn't come."

"I am going to be late!
My story will be ruined . . .

and that's why I'm crying."

"Well, I'm a wolf.
I'm pitch black.
And I have big teeth.
If you like, I can help you."

The little girl looked at him
with tears in her eyes.
"You would do that for me?"

"Yes," answered the wolf. "I have all the time in the world."
"Would you come with me to Grandmother's house?
On our way there, I'll tell you what to do."
"All right!"

And so off they went, arm-in-arm, walking toward Grandmother's house.
On the road, they parted ways to begin the story.
"Don't forget your disguise!" said the little girl.

"Don't worry," answered the wolf. "I know what to do . . ."